DID YOU HEAR ME?
A LIFE IN THE WEEK OF HARVEY

By: Laura Olsen

Harvey has a lot of issues and everyone else don't really help.
This book deals with mental illness and contains topics that others may find triggering such as death, depression, suicide, self-harm, substance abuse, and mild violence.

Part One:
Monday
.SadSam.

Waking up in his own bed, in his own clothes, in his own head, Sam was grateful to be staring at the speckled pattern on the ceiling. He could see a warped spot in the paint where water leaked in; in but not through. His chest lifted with a breath and deflated.

Grateful.

What an odd sensation.

To be awake again.

To be feeling like this again.

It wasn't that he didn't like being awake, he just merely didn't like *being*. Out in the front. Out in the open. Their world was a forever spinning cycle of misery and he was at the wheel again. Who made that decision? Who took a look at all the players and thought, "yeah, Sam should be the one in charge." He didn't know what he was doing. He didn't know what any of them were doing. He just did what he could to get through the day.

In but not through.

Was that thought counter intuitive or counterproductive? Jenn would know. She would say, "how is this helping anything? How is feeling sorry for yourself in any way positive or good?"

Positive or good.

Odd concepts. Old concepts. Words used by younger men who didn't know the true length of toil. How it wears on you.

He stretched and felt his muscles pull and relax around his frame, he was tired, his stomach hurt and there was a little bit of acid reflux still hanging out towards the top of his sternum. How it *wears* on you.

Jenn would say, turn your attention to what you can do to make things better. To make things different. A feeling is just a feeling, it doesn't have to define you. It doesn't have to be your state of being. So what should he do? He was awake, after all, he could be doing something. He *should* be doing something. It was just a matter of what would be the most beneficial to the unit. What would carry them forward? He could set aside the placid feeling of depression and work towards a better tomorrow. He could reduce the inner turmoil to just words in the back of his mind and get to the actual physical act of living. Words were just words.

Words and stuff and things.

He closed his eyes and wondered if he could go back to sleep, let this day pass by like all the other days. There would be more days, more time to do more things. It didn't have to be today, there was nothing saying that anything had to happen today.

But there's so much to do.

The thought sung through him like an electric current of anxiety, resting as a pang of guilt in his empty stomach. He had to get moving. Had to do his part. Everyone had a part to play in this hellacious nightmare of a life and he wasn't pulling his weight if he wasn't doing his part. Laying in bed and moaning about right and wrong and this and that and whose turn it was to carry them forward wasn't actually getting them anywhere. Reduce the noise. Reduce the feelings. Fold them neatly in a box and put them back where you found them.

Sam swung his legs over the side of the bed and got to his feet. His right hip cracked and his knees popped in accordance. He was getting older, he couldn't keep waking up like this. He couldn't keep doing this. He was supposed to be done . He was supposed to have an easy life. He was supposed to be allowed to go home.

But there's so much to do.

Walking from the bedroom to the kitchen, he had to watch his step to avoid the garbage and dirty clothes strewn about. He wished he knew where his slippers were, then he wouldn't have to feel the grit in the carpet on his naked feet. He spotted a sock in one area and put it on, a little bit of digging later and he'd acquired another sock. Feeling marginally better, he continued his quest for coffee. Rank smells, multiple, wafted from the living room and the kitchen. He fought the desire to go back to bed. At least in bed he didn't have to see what state they were living in. At least in bed, he could close his eyes and pretend that everything he did always stayed the same and he wasn't running on a constant, endless, hamster wheel, never making a difference. Never getting anywhere. He wanted to die. But he wasn't allowed to die.

Mike left the TV on again all night, the loading screen of a popular game softly emitted music and shadows danced across old plates of food and empty beer cans. The sound swelled in his mind and he felt the ever present hatred coming to the surface. Hatred was never a good feeling. Never a positive feeling. But Sam hated Mike. He cleared his throat and shifted his focus away, trying to ignore it. Mike wasn't his problem. Mike wasn't his responsibility. Harvey brought Mike into their lives and it was Harvey's job to take Mike out of their lives. But he would never leave. It seemed he'd been with them for an eternity. Always this glowing ember of addiction and self destruction, always this light in a dark tunnel that smelled of fire and blood and death. Harvey wouldn't give him up, not for anything.

It was hard getting through to Harvey. It was like he wasn't there most of the time. Empty air where thoughts should have been. No emotions, no effort. Harvey was more than content to let his life get away from him and all of them could see it. They could see inside, even feel, deep down what was in his soul, but no one could get through. No one could actually wake him up enough to get him moving.

In but not through.

Was this a losing battle? Was this a lost cause? Was all the effort, all the work, was it all for nothing? Sam cleared just enough dirty dishes out of the way to start a pot of coffee and left it to brew while he went to relieve himself in the bathroom. He sighed and felt his shoulders stiffen as his socked foot suddenly became cold and damp. He looked at the urine speckling the floor and the toilet seat. Mike couldn't pee in the bowl when he'd been drinking. Or maybe he didn't even try. Sam wouldn't put that past him. Mike was lazy and selfish and cared about one agenda and one agenda alone: escaping reality.

Maybe that's why Harvey relied on him so much. Harvey hated reality so much, it was more than avoidance, it was almost as if he was trying to obliterate it completely. Mike helped with that. There were no rules in his world. No right or wrong. There was desire and there was obtaining that which he desired. He existed outside of reality and Harvey existed there with him.

As if to punctuate this thought, Sam saw Twenty-Thousand Leagues Under the Sea by Jules Vern resting on the edge of the bathtub, cigarette butts stuffed into one of Jenn's coffee mugs sitting next to it. At least there were signs of life from Harvey.

At some point in time he sat in the tub and read his favorite book. Sam found that to be a hopeful thought, it boosted his mood a little bit. He didn't know where Harvey was this morning but at some point in time he'd been reading and that was important.

Of course, Sam reminded himself, Harvey needed to do a lot more than just pull himself out of bed to read in the bathtub. A terrorist's proof of life was not the same thing as a healthy sign of movement.

Jenn was going to be upset about the mug. But when wasn't she upset about anything? She was very good at griping and making her disappointment with the entire situation known. She hated Harvey smoking. She hated him smoking in the apartment, she hated him smoking outside. She hated the smell, the taste, the cost. She hated all of it and yet, Harvey's bad habit persisted.

Sam flushed the toilet and went to the sink to wash his hands. His gaze avoided the mirror, he didn't want to see what he knew he was going to see. Time was getting away from everyone. Life was getting away from everyone. They had to do something. They had to help Harvey.

Help Harvey.

How could he help Harvey? Sam had been trying to help him his whole life and with everyone reaching their thirties, it was hard to imagine a life where Harvey didn't need his help. It seemed like Harvey needed him more and more every day. Every day he sunk further and further away from the land of the living.

Employment.

Sam knew Harvey always did better with a job, the activity, the structure, it kept him grounded and here and in person. But it was so hard for him to consistently wake up and go to a job. If he was scheduled a Monday-Friday, he might be there two out of the five days then… just stop trying. Something would happen, someone would say something and Harvey would have to find Mike and drink about it for a few days.

He always had to get away from life. From this life. From this horrible broken mess of a life. Sam cleared off a spot at the dining room table for his laptop and opened one of the several job sourcing websites he'd bookmarked last week.

If he could find Harvey a job, maybe Harvey could find the will to do more than what he was doing at the present moment. Jenn would call this *hope*. Sam wasn't sure if he would call it anything than just moving forward. Doing what he could to make sure Harvey had a fighting chance, even if he didn't want to fight for himself.

They were all trying to fight for Harvey, even Mike in all of his alcoholic idiocy, he was even trying to fight for Harvey. So where was Harvey?

Life doesn't have to be this hard, Harvey.

Sam looked over Harvey's short resume and tried to remember a time when he felt like Harvey had more to offer. He did, didn't he? Harvey had talent, Harvey had uses, Harvey had a purpose. He was more than this resume, Sam reminded himself. He was more than an old book and a mug of cigarette butts. He was a whole person.

A whole person. You're a whole person, Harvey.

Harvey had a degree in graphic design, he was capable and creative. He needed to get out of bed and apply himself to his life. Still, Sam looked for the easy jobs. The dishwashers, the busboys. Jobs that didn't require too much from Harvey, just enough for him to bring something good and substantial to the table. Something that made him feel… like he'd earned another day.

Sam was tired. He wanted to go back to sleep. He was done with this day and he never really even started it. The apartment was quiet and empty. Lonely, almost. More often than not, he enjoyed it this way but sometimes the desire for companionship cropped up and he felt the same dull ache in his chest that he always got.

His mind wandered to the forbidden topic of Aurora. He knew it was forbidden for a reason. She was as off-limits as any subject could be in this apartment but no one else was around so what was the harm? He wondered if she thought of him. Or any of them, really. She'd been such an important figure in their world for so long it was hard to think that their time together was over but Sam forced himself to do it all the same. Visualize her absence, feel it.

The ache in his chest receded.

She was gone and she wasn't coming back.

Harvey did so much better with Aurora around. She was the light in his eyes and everyone knew it. Then she left and the light went out. It never came back on after that. Jenn came around less. Mike came around more and Harvey… well. Harvey couldn't really handle it, could he?

They all loved Aurora in their own ways but Sam knew it was nothing compared to what Harvey felt. Aurora was Harvey's first and only love. The love of his life, as he wrote it, over and over again in not the best of poetry. Harvey wasn't a writer but when Aurora left, he penned pages and pages. It was like his heart was exploding and the only thing he could do was write without ceasing for hours on end.

Finally losing her calm, Aurora's otherwise dark eyes flashed with anger and frustration, "Harvey! I can't do this anymore! I need to be able to be my own person!"

And that's when Harvey fell to the floor and never got back up. They needed her to come back. They needed her to help get Harvey off the floor. But Sam knew Aurora better than that. And what Jenn would label as *hope,* Sam would call delusional. Harvey was too much for Aurora, he was too much for most people. He needed to learn to be strong on his own; she had to be let go because he was drowning her. He was choking the life out of the only person who'd ever looked at Harvey and saw something substantial.

With that thought, Sam decided to do the laundry. Harvey needed clean clothes if he had any interviews and it was a good thing to do. It made him feel good. Productive.

Sam picked up various items of clothing from around the apartment ranging from comfortable to business casual, hoping to give Harvey a few choices to pick through later on when he decided to get moving.

Always plan for a future and there will be a future.

A motto Sam relied on often to get him through his day to day. Always plan for a future and there will be a future. That future might just be this load of laundry, but it was a future nonetheless. It was the metaphorical putting one foot in front of the other. It was moving forward, a place Harvey desperately needed to be.

Sam closed the lid on the washer and leaned heavily on the appliance, feeling his resolve begin to falter and fall away. He took a deep breath, he needed to at least finish this load of laundry. He needed to at least get through the rest of the afternoon. He could do it. He could wade through the sudden wave of listlessness that inundated his senses. He was floating away or free falling. Vertigo pulled him to the floor and Sam laid there, prone for some time, the world spinning silently around him. He closed his eyes and tried to concentrate on the comforting sound of the washer going through its cycles.

He thought about the cigarette butts in the coffee cup and he thought about his own coffee sitting on the dining room table next to his laptop. These were all real, physical things that he could visualize and focus on. He felt the episode subside and he quietly moved to a sitting position with his back firmly against the wall, his knees hugged almost to his chest.

Time passed and the washer completed its cycle, signaling Sam to move the clothes over to the dryer. He got to his feet and swallowed residual nausea. He moved the clothes from the washer to the dryer and promptly decided he needed to get something to eat.

It'd been a while since he'd eaten anything and none of them had gone grocery shopping recently. Besides, venturing out might be good for him. Get him out of this apartment, away from these feelings, and let him just breathe for a moment.

*

This is annoying. Mike thought petulantly as he drummed his fingers on the steering wheel of his car, third in line for them to even take his order. And he still had to stop at the gas station for smokes and something to drink.

He checked the balance on the debit card and made a face. He was definitely going to order more food than what that number allowed. Practical Sam would bitch but Mike couldn't care less, to be honest. Honestly, fuck this whole thing. This whole reality was a dumpster fire of misery. If Sam didn't want him to have a couple extra burritos then fuck him. He wasn't doing shit as far as Mike was concerned. He just wandered around aimlessly all day and bitched.

Him and Jenn, bitch and moan and nag.

Mike ordered his food, making sure to order extra for Harvey later that night, and handed the cashier the emergency credit card. Food was like an emergency. Food was definitely an emergency. He told himself the same thing when he bought a carton for himself and Harvey to share as well as an eighteen pack of beer.

Maybe Sam just hadn't tried being not sober. Maybe Sam just didn't know that they could turn it off for a while. All of it. Everything. You can forget the whole world is burning down around you if you really want to.

Mike loved returning to a quiet, empty apartment. He shook the stress out of his shoulders and took the beer and food to the kitchen, getting ready for another night by himself. Well, not really by himself. Harvey would be around sooner or later and he had his squad.

Mike booted up his gaming console and the tv, located his headset amidst the trash around his chair, and was ready to get the night underway.

He connected to the lobby and noted that his friends were already all there. Perfect, good. He didn't have to wait for anyone. They could just get started. No one had to make small talk, no one had to ask him how he was doing. No one had to ask him how his day was or why it'd been long. He could just be a voice on a headset. No responsibilities, no priorities. Having already shotgunned two beers earlier in the kitchen to prepare himself, Mike held his third beer of the night up to his microphone and popped the tab.

"ASMR, quality content," he half-whispered, taking a full gulp.

There was a chorus of chuckles and hellos as everyone recognized him and Mike sunk back into the comfort of being in a different space for a while, forgetting about the trash cradling his person.

When is the fucking sun going to exist again?

Part Two:
Tuesday

.morning.

Mike kept his eyes closed, trying to block out the realization that he was in the bathtub again.
He was always waking up in the bathtub. What was so special about the fucking bathtub? Aurora used to say it had to do with anxiety and security and a lost sense of self. "Fuck Aurora." He outwardly grumbled while he moved to a more sitting position, taking in the wreckage around him from the night before.

He looked down at his shirt, that was in fact Sam's shirt, and noted it was smeared with either old burrito or old vomit, he couldn't rightly tell. Yet another thing for Sam to bitch about. Oh well. He rubbed his face with both hands and tried to think through the lingering brain fog that always came with being awake.

He was doing his part, wasn't he? Weren't they all just doing their part for Harvey? Harvey. Where was Harvey this morning? He'd been home last night but only long for him to drink too much and puke all over the toilet. Other than that he was virtually MIA. But that's the way Harvey liked it. He kept his own hours and those hours he kept to himself.

That was the way of Harvey and that was why Mike was here, so that the others wouldn't overwhelm him. At his core, Harvey was delicate and prone to disaster if pushed too hard. Sam and Jenn didn't get that. Especially Sam.

Get up, Harvey. Get a job, Harvey.

Harvey was doing his fucking best just to stay alive. Maybe Sam should get up and get a job. Had he ever thought of that? No, he hadn't because Sam was a putz. "Putz." Mike said the word out loud, it even sounded like Sam. He said it again, this time deepening his voice and really annunciating the word,

"Putz."

Rude.

Mike felt a tug. A pull. A woozy sensation he would not label welcoming. That meant it was time for one thing and one thing only: morning beer.

He pulled himself from the bathtub and tossed the soiled shirt onto the floor before grabbing a cleanish one from a full basket. Morning beers always hit a little better than afternoon beers. Afternoon beers were born out of frustration and grief. Morning beers were beautiful creatures coming to fill you up and give you life all day before the hangover from the night before could set in.

He loved morning beers.

Harvey loved morning beers.

Sam and Jenn should really try morning beers.

"Huh." Mike uttered aloud as he realized there wasn't anything left in the fridge. Harvey had come and gone and taken more than Mike thought. He told himself he didn't mind it. Harvey needed what Harvey needed but Mike was still peeved he now had to go out before he could settle in for another day of doing absolutely nothing.

A trip through the drive-thru and a stop at the gas station later and Mike was successfully back at home, logged on and ready to fucking get back at it.

The sun was going down through the shades and Mike still hadn't touched the fast food he'd bought himself hours before. He'd lost track of the time between rounds and was only roused back to the land of the living by the rather intense need to urinate.

Stumbling to the bathroom, he caught sight of himself in the mirror and felt his stomach turn over. He avoided mirrors for a reason and he didn't want to have to deal with that reason tonight. His whole point was to not deal with anything. He was the suspension of reality...or so he told himself as he steadied his body with one hand firmly clutching the shower curtain, trying to pee anywhere but on his person.

He just didn't want to have to deal with the uncertainty of it all. Couldn't Sam get that? Couldn't Sam figure it out for himself? If he was so fucking smart, why couldn't he understand that there was no possible way any of them were going to save Harvey so they may as well just let Harvey have a good time?

Harvey's not having a good time.

They just needed to get with the program, get on board. Making Harvey get a job wasn't helping Harvey. It was reminding Harvey what he could and couldn't do. Dishwasher? Busboy? Is that really what Sam thought all Harvey was capable of? Couldn't he see he was just tearing Harvey down? Cutting him off at the knees? Telling him to get off the fucking floor but not giving him anywhere to go.

Sometimes you gotta just let things be as they are. Harvey clearly wasn't ready to do whatever Sam wanted him to do and Sam needed to respect that. Harvey had boundaries. Sam needed to respect Harvey's boundaries. And frankly, Mike wasn't going to argue about it anymore. He flushed the toilet and stumbled away from the mirror and the bathroom and everything else he was avoiding, feeling more resolved than ever, satisfied in his small emotional rant against everyone else.

He was going to enjoy himself. No matter what sort of negativity Jenn and Sam brought to the table, he was going to make sure he did his part and took care of Harvey.

Number one, what they really needed was a rowing machine. He was tired of everyone walking around with slumped, lazy shoulders. If everyone just worked on building a backbone maybe they could get somewhere, finally.

Number two, this apartment was suffocating Harvey. They needed to change something. They needed to move stuff around, maybe? Give everyone a clean space to think. Of course none of them could get along, how could they in this filth? Jesus, didn't anyone clean around here?

Trash bags. He needed trash bags. He knew he was stumbling. But was he really? What was connection to this world from the next? Was it stumbling if it wasn't falling? Was side stepping just as valid a movement as any other?

He didn't shake the smirk from his face like he knew he should. He didn't stop himself from spreading his lips, exposing his teeth and twisting one foot in the kitchen, right hand landing on the fridge's handle and pulling the door open with a flourish.

"We're going to do this right, Harvey. And we're going to do it our way." He said, selecting one of the last cans.

He still had plenty of time before Jenn got home.

They could buy new plates, he decided. And utensils. And glass pans. Harvey's mom was an expert at estate sales. They could get all this stuff on the cheap. What they really needed was a fresh start.

With that thought in mind, he set his beer can down on the counter and swayed ever so slightly forward.

He turned his focus to the stupid white board Jenn hung up for a quick messages. He mostly used it for phallic artistry but this time he felt like being constructive.

FIND A BETTER PLACE TO LIVE.
THIS PLACE IS A SHIT HOLE.

Satisfied with the message, he fumbled with the cap on the marker, it dropped to the floor and Mike made a face. He put the marker back, sans cap. *'Everything is replaceable.'*

He filled bag after bag. Stacked them in a neat pile in the middle of the living room. He envisioned setting them ablaze and just letting this world burn away. Reduce the noise and chaos to a smoldering heap of debris. Never to produce anything worth condemnation ever again.

But the neighbors downstairs would complain again- so it was probably in everyone's best interests if he did not.

Instead he went back to the fridge and underlined his message. Unsteady legs and heavy shoulders stooped down and found the cap to the marker, putting it back before he caused any real damage.

"Other people matter." Aurora's smile was soft. It was always soft, *"you gotta think about them too."*

Against his will, almost, it seemed, Mike found himself conceding to the old memory. Sometimes. Sometimes things mattered.

Sometimes.

He needed to take the garbage outside. He couldn't just leave it there. Who else was gonna do it? Sam? Mike rolled his eyes, "putz."

Trip after trip, Mike moved back and forth, emptying the apartment of its filth. Jenn could do the little stuff, he didn't really care. He was doing his part. Harvey would be home soon and they'd relax for a bit.

Things were never as dire as them seemed, sometimes you just needed to get the garbage out of the house.

As Mike's last act of kindness for the night he started the damp load in the dryer Sam left from the day before. Harvey would appreciate clean clothes.

Part Three:
Wednesday & Thursday
.Respectively, reserved for you.

Jenn stared with a forlorn look at her appearance in the mirror. She pulled the skin down below her left eye and leaned in close just to get a real good look at how blood shot and exhausted they really were. When was the last time she slept? When was the last time she remembered going to sleep? She sighed, what a rabbit hole she didn't feel like going down that morning.

Or ever, really. She was tired of this life. This merciless caricature of what living was. She didn't want to be a part of it anymore. She didn't want to be around anymore. She removed herself time and time again, only to wind up back here. Back in this same place, doing the same things, catering to the same toxic behaviors.

Her face was puffy and her gut, although empty and growling for nutrition, was bloated, distended from empty wheat-filled calories. She tried to square her shoulders and straighten her posture, if only to improve her overall appearance a fraction of the way. But the weight of the world pulled harder than any confidence she could muster and she stared at the slump.

She felt like a mockery. A fool. A fraud. Standing in this body that was not her body, she tried to find the resolve she knew was in there somewhere. Somewhere she could swallow all these feelings and do what had to be done. How many times had she done it in the past? She didn't need sleep. She didn't need to eat. She needed to move.

Jenn forcefully pushed herself away from the bathroom countertop, she didn't want to look at it anymore. Her face. Her body. Her life.

She knew someone had to. Someone had to take inventory. Someone had to take charge. So she did it. Because someone had to. Who else was going to? Harvey? Usually optimistic about Harvey's progress, Jenn just couldn't muster it that morning. Harvey recovering seemed like such a far off idea. Everyday it slipped further and further away.

Didn't any of them realize this was why she didn't want to come home anymore? All of this, it was always left up to her. How was that okay? How was that right? She shouldn't always have to deal with this. It *wasn't* right.

Was this just her role now? Did they think it was her sole purpose? She was so much more than this. She was so much more capable.

Nevertheless, she grabbed a blue bandana from the floor and pushed her greasy brown hair back, getting it out of her face. She stripped the sheets from Harvey's bed and started a fresh load of linens. In the flurry of movement, a cloud of body odor assaulted her senses. She'd have to take a shower when this was all over. It was only right. It would have to be the last thing on the list; at least it looked like there were clean clothes in the dryer for her to wear. So that was something. She gathered the rest of the clothes into baskets and lined them up neatly, ready to be washed. Hopefully she'd have time to get them.

She folded the load in the dryer and set aside clean shorts and a t-shirt for herself. For the after. For when her work was finished and she was allowed to take a shower.

Jenn took in the general disarray of the apartment and sighed. Maybe if Sam vacuumed instead of applied for jobs that Harvey wouldn't take, they'd all be a little better off. Maybe Mike was right, maybe they all should just leave Harvey alone. Let him sink in that derelict ship and let it all go.

The note on the fridge caught her eye almost immediately. Of course. Of course that would be Mike's contribution.

In her own feminine scrawl she wrote a response, not really caring how it came across to anyone else.

<u>FIND A BETTER PLACE TO LIVE</u>
<u>THIS PLACE IS A SHIT HOLE</u>
Maybe you could help with that or something.

Looking around the kitchen she noticed most of the dishes were gone. Just gone. Not piled somewhere or maybe in the dishwasher, even. Just gone. Vanished. No longer a part of this mortal coil. Naturally, this meant Mike "did the dishes." His sporadic contributions to the wellness of their unit always ended up being more expensive than just doing whatever it was he didn't want to do. They couldn't afford to replace all these dishes. They could barely afford to keep their lights on. She wished he'd stop drinking. She wished he'd stop encouraging Harvey to drink. They just made dumb decisions and set everyone back three paces without even meaning to. She knew he meant well. She knew this was his version of trying to help. But it wasn't helping. And how was she supposed to convey that?

She closed her eyes and willed away the desire to text Aurora. Ask her for help again. Ask her to come over and laugh and make everything okay again. Make the dirt and grime make sense. When Aurora was around, Jenn felt like it was okay to like herself. Not just accept herself but like herself. And she knew that's what Harvey felt. That's why he took it so hard when she said she had to take a step back. For her own sake. The void it caused was a black hole that stole so much more than any of them knew. But it had to happen. It had to. They'd all relied on one person too much. This was their penance. The universe holding them accountable and she knew, as was with most self-inflicted suffering, there was a possible road to absolution.

Contacting Aurora now was a purely selfish motivation serving only to make Jenn feel better. That didn't respect Aurora's autonomy, which was the center of the last of their arguments before she left.

Her gaze shifted to the collection of dirty coffee mugs corralled in the corner of the counter top. No matter how gross they got, Mike never threw them away… Jenn told herself this was because he knew they were important to her. They weren't things he would consider 'replaceable.' She took this as a small comfort. It was unusually kind of him, very uncharacteristic of one of Mike's mood shifts from passive to proactive. This small comfort she felt was used as fuel to actually wash and put away the coffee cups. Seeing them in the cupboard, ready, waiting, and clean made her feel like things could better again. They had to get better again.

Again, Jenn had to think, was anything they were doing really helping Harvey? In the grand scheme of things? Did Harvey even want to be helped? That was the big question-- the looming words of doom that floated atop their small world in big bold letters.

Did Harvey even want to be helped?

She shook her mindset back towards her resolve and tackled the stove, removing the burners, lifting the top and scrubbing underneath. Taking the time to set the oven to self-clean. They needed to save money by making meals at home. Not going out to get fast food whenever they were hungry enough to care to eat. This meant they had to have a clean work space. She'd give that to them. That was her part. Her contribution. She told herself to complain less, to look forward more. Every action was a step towards harmonious cohabitation.

This was helping Harvey, not speculation, not self-pitying prose. Proactive movements towards a higher quality of life.

The fridge was terrifying, to say the least, there were meals in there from months prior. Good months, happy months, months where they cared enough to prepare meals. She held her breath as she scraped the old contents from various food containers into a trash bag. Why was this always her job? Why couldn't anyone else do this? She remembered Mike's solution of throwing away the dishes and sighed. Better her than him.

What a disaster.

Jenn was surprised they had enough dishes left to fill the entire dishwasher and set it to the hottest cycle. That meant cleanest… right?

She made a mixture of bleach and soap water in the sink and proceeded to wipe out the shelves in the fridge, taking the time to check the expiration dates on the condiments in the door and discard the old ones. This was good. This was a good thing that was happening. It was good that she was doing this.

By the time she was done with the kitchen it was late in the evening and her poor sleeping habits were getting the best of her. She needed to rest.

Jenn shuffled into bed, sighing heavily when she realized she forgot the sheets in the dryer. That's alright, she told herself, she would wake up tomorrow morning and get back at it. She still had to do the living room and the bathroom. She had time tomorrow. This was just a slight intermission. There was always tomorrow.

Thursday came swiftly and as promised.

Jenn awoke. Feeling the bare mattress against her skin, waking up in her own bed, in her own head, Jenn was grateful to be staring at the speckled pattern on the ceiling. Grateful.

It was a good day for it to be a Thursday. She had more energy, she had more resolve. Less of whatever negativity she was carrying around with her yesterday. Those feelings weren't her fight. She didn't need them clouding up her thought space. She knew who she was. She knew her purpose. And there were a lot of things she had to get done today. She began by sitting at the clean kitchen table and making a list of her tasks for the day. She only had so many hours and she had to make the most of them.

The bathroom was a warzone. Multiple days of Harvey and Mike tag teaming the toilet was something she had to contend with before anything else. She shook her head, such a thankless task. It'd just be the same next week, maybe worse depending on how the weekend went. Her mind wandered briefly to the time Mike flushed a lighter down the toilet. It got stuck in the u bend and the clog caused the toilet to overflow while Mike was sleeping. The water seeped through the neighbor's ceiling below them and that's who actually alerted the building maintenance to the problem. They were still paying off the repairs.

Jenn thought that'd be when Mike and Harvey would learn their lesson but alas, it was not. If anything, it seemed to increase the rate of their decline. Any facade of self control or will power went out the window, what they wanted, they did. And that usually meant nothing productive but chain smoke cigarettes and drink. And there she always was, cleaning up after them.

She had to take a scouring stick to the sink to get it all the way clean. Weeks of built up toothpaste, spit into the basin, not bothered to be rinsed down the drain, had turned into mint scented cement and again, Jenn felt that resentfulness from yesterday. This was ridiculous. Just utterly ridiculous.

When a chunk of debris pierced her nail bed for the third time she made what Aurora once dubbed 'her angry muppet noise,' a high pitched growl in the back of her throat, more cartoonish than menacing, and closed her eyes, pushing the negative feelings down. She had to help Harvey. And being mad at him wasn't helping him. Cleaning the sink helped him. Cleaning the sink was something she could do.

Proactive instead of passive. That's how they were going to help Harvey. That's how they were going to crawl out of this mess.

Having put their living conditions in order, Jenn set her sights on the other matters needing attention. Not Sam's obsession with Harvey's employment, not Mike's escapism. Reality.

A wave of nausea rippled through her and Jenn lost her balance. She shifted her weight to her heels, flattening her feet against the ground and felt herself push into the floor. She visualized the floor connected to the earth, following the path from her feet in the carpet to the support beams, running into the foundation. The foundation connected to the earth, the solid, stable, earth. She stood there for a moment with her eyes closed, feeling solid, feeling connected, an exercise her therapist taught her, and stayed in control of the moment.

But time had passed and Jenn became aware of the disconcerting silence in the apartment, washer and dryer long done with their cycles.

The sun outside was lower in the sky, the night approaching the day, the sky blushing a light rose from it's cool kiss.

There was so much else she could have done. Jenn knew this, but still, she chose to sit at the kitchen table. Curious fingers crawled across the table and quietly tapped in the unlock code for Harvey's phone. He kept it on the table for emergencies. Jenn wouldn't call this an emergency… she only wanted to see. Only wanted to know. Only wanted to sate her curiosity and maybe heal a little bit of this misery she could no longer ignore.

She hovered over the old familiar social media app for a second before fully making her decision. She knew it wasn't good for her. This wasn't good for anyone in the apartment. Aurora was off limits. She was the forever forbidden subject. But Jenn missed her too and her feelings were just as valid as Harvey's. Her feelings were as valid as anyone's.

And what would be the harm in saying that? What would it hurt to just say, "hey, thinking of you, miss you. Hope you're taking care."

Jenn rolled the idea around in her head and thought about whether or not it could come across as manipulative. She didn't want to manipulate Aurora's feelings. She just wanted to say she missed her.

Communication is manipulation.

Jenn's shoulders shook out the feelings of guilt in regards to the idea she was posing. It might not be a bad idea, later. It might come out that it was a great idea. Maybe Aurora was just waiting for one of them to say something. To come around and tell her that they missed her.

Cold, damp, hands typed the text and hit sent before any more thoughts could talk her out of it. She needed to say it, she needed to be able to express it.

It didn't matter if Aurora said anything back or not, she knew now, that Jenn was there and thinking of her and maybe that was enough. With a punctuated swallow, Jenn resolved herself to let it be enough.

She scrolled through the rest of Aurora's newer content. There were faces, names she didn't recognize. Jokes she didn't get. These are the people Aurora replaced them with. New friends. Better friends. Friends that didn't require a great amount of mental fortitude. Regular, ordinary, friends.

Everyone's replaceable.

Jenn felt herself bristling more and more. Becoming less open than she was before, her earlier, selfless desire of only wanting Aurora's happiness was quickly being replaced by that same resentment, nipping at her heels for the last two days. Chasing her down, finding her when she was vulnerable. She didn't want to be replaced. She didn't want to be seen as replaceable. She wasn't! She wasn't the one that fucked everything up!

Jenn tried to squash the sudden malice she felt towards Harvey. But it was the actual, awful, truth and she was tired of being punished for something that wasn't her fault! She loved Aurora too! Maybe not in the same way as Harvey but their relationship was still valid. It still counted. Didn't it? Didn't she count? Didn't she matter?

STOP.

Jenn cut the internal rant short with a sharp breath in. This wasn't proactive. This wasn't the goal. This was not forward motion. How would this make Harvey feel later? How would this affect him?

Tomorrow's not promised, there are no absolutes. It was too late, the damage was done, it was there, out in the open for everyone to see. So she felt nothing when she sent the next line.

"Why don't you miss me?"

Part Four:
Friday
.hello harvey.

Where are
you, Harvey?

Are you home? Are you here?

Can you
hear me, Harvey?

There was a sound within a sound.

A murmur.

A
gathering of
starlings.

They stuck to the trees and paid no mind to him.

Or maybe he was a part of them. A collection of something that resulted in a whisper.

He was too big, a hulking mass, bulky frame. Too large. The softness became paradoxical and therefore comical.

Drowning in a blue sea, it seemed.

Experienci
ng
homesickn
ess.

He watched bubbles shimmer to the surface. Dizzying fractures of light beckoned for him to follow. He inhaled the kaleidoscope of colors and sunk further into the darkness of the deep, letting the murmur be.

Harvey rubbed his face. The light peeking through the blinds told him it was day time, more specifically, morning. He could feel clean sheets underneath him and the faint scent of bleach somewhere. He knew where he was. He knew who he was. He was awake and he was alive. Thankfully, gratefully, the birds were not chirping.

Okay sure, but what day is it again?

His legs stuttered across the carpet as he suspiciously eyed the floors and their lack of garbage. He hadn't slept that long. Also, not that hard. In the bathroom he found a pile of his clothes, waiting next to some fresh towels. *That was nice.* He could feel the dirt stuck to the oils on his skin, feel the plaque on his teeth against the inside of his lips. He absentmindedly itched his scalp. A shower wasn't a bad idea.

Harvey made his way to the kitchen to start a pot of coffee. One foot in front of the other. Forward motion. On his way past the fridge, without turning his head, Harvey balled up his fist and swiped through the letters; eliminating half of the words before he processed what they said. Nonsense. That's all that was. Voices screaming into the void. Obnoxious.

He swallowed and grabbed the marker. Penned his own thought and left it at that. Three words that weren't all that complicated.
let me die

It was a decision he was content to make. He wasn't going to bring about his demise but he also wasn't going to stop it either. They needed to figure that out. Get on board. He was only a fraction of a person. Never really quite able to attain full autonomy. Hollywood would call this an extra. His therapist would call this unhealthy.

He'd rather be extra.

Lukewarm left overs.

There was a peace in this acceptance. A calm sort of gray area where one realized that nothing actually mattered. When you die, you die. And if people are going to remember you, they're going to remember you. But they're going to die too. And so- the memory of you, or the memories of you, will reach an end and with it, the shame of your existence. He was ready to get to that part of the story. Of his story.

While the coffee brewed, he saw his phone on the table had been disturbed from its usual docked position. A point of interest that lit up parts of his brain with glowing orange bolts of anxiety. He sucked air in through clenched teeth. He needed to change his lock code. But what good would it do? He wasn't allowed privacy. He wasn't allowed space or boundaries. What was his was never really his. He was a collection of missing pieces. More pitiful than grotesque.

Harvey turned his attention to the cupboard above the coffee maker and opened it with a sigh. He could eat ramen. Aurora was always going on and on about how it wasn't really food, just wax and flavored salt, but it kept. And so he kept with it. When he went for a bowl, his quest came up short. Where were the dishes? For a moment, he allowed himself to become confused and move from cupboard to cupboard, checking each twice for what he knew wasn't there. He slammed the last cupboard shut. What did it matter if there were no dishes? What use was there for dishes in the grand scheme of things? Animals didn't need dishes. Dead men didn't need dishes.

He filled a mug with black coffee. It wasn't like he hadn't existed on coffee for days before. He was used to it. Helped him keep up his disappointing physique. He sipped it until he was more sick to his stomach than hungry.

Settling down in front of his laptop, he pulled open the browser history. Job sites again. There were numbers in red bubbles on the tabs. Employers had responded, waiting for his response. He let out a deep exhale, that was a hard pass. It wasn't that he didn't want employment… yes it was. He had to be honest with himself, someone had to. Harvey this. Harvey that. Move Harvey forward.

He itched his scalp again, he needed that shower. He could feel his skin crawling, begging to be scrubbed clean. But there was no use he told himself. There was no point. He'd just need another shower in a few days.

He'd just need another job in a few months.

A different tab pulled his attention away. Someone had been where they weren't supposed to be. Breaking rules. Nothing was sacred here.

There was her face, bright. Beautiful. She looked a lot better than the last time he'd seen her. Then she'd been crying. She'd been crying for days. Her eyes were puffy, swollen from the salt water that seeped out in her sleep.

She'd said she couldn't bear it anymore. She'd bookmarked several articles on caregiver fatigue before she left. He would never tell her, he'd already read them, found them on his own. He saw it before she did. That's why he didn't beg her to stay. That's why he wouldn't beg now.

Aurora had done her time, put in her work, and he wasn't going to take any more from her. He wasn't going to break her. Not the way he broke everything else. Aurora needed her own life. She needed to be able to live it. That was his decision.

But still, the feeling persisted. The ache. The wish that things hadn't turned out the way they did. He envisioned a different future. A whole future. One that didn't have nightmares ebbing at the corners, monsters lurking just out of sight.

Harvey felt a pang of nausea and sipped more coffee, cementing the gut rot. This was the way things had to be.

She accused him of not trying. Her patience with his growing apathy was wearing thin. She demanded to know how many appointments he had canceled versus how many had accidentally been "lost."

"This isn't just your life, Harvey!" she shouted, "this is our life! Mine and yours together! And what are you doing?"

"Nothing." Harvey whispered out loud at the memory, "nothing."

There was an emptiness in his honesty. The truth no longer mattered. The confession no longer yielded absolution. But still, his life persisted.

He closed the tab and slammed his laptop shut. No. He wasn't going to do this to himself anymore. Aurora made her choice and he didn't blame her. He couldn't hold it against her. He knew their odds and he knew she tried her hardest. It just didn't work.

Was it ever going to work? Not likely.

But maybe he should take that shower.

*

He had to hand it to Jenn, she did a great job on the apartment, Mike thought as he loaded the fridge with another case of beer, settling in for a nice weekend. He even stopped at the grocery store and got some frozen pizzas. That helped, right? Harvey didn't even notice half the work Jenn put in and he was pissed at Sam so it was up to Mike to save the day.

Always saving the day. Always swoopin' in and scoopin' up the pieces. They weren't helping Harvey. They made him feel worse. Inadequate. Incomplete.

"Who needs bowls, Jenn?" Mike asked out loud to the empty apartment. No one. Harvey was gonna figure his shit out. It was fine. Everything was going to be fine.

Moving to the living room he settled in for a long night of doing nothing. He sank into his chair and let out a contented sigh. The apartment was clean, wasn't it? They all did a little laundry, also good. They were moving forward. Slow and steady wins the race.

Logging on, he saw the names on the screen. Faceless names, things he could connect with just enough to take off the ebb of loneliness. At least it was some form of personal connection. Hard thing to find these days when interpersonal connection was so complicated. Everything was something else that needed to be deciphered. People became puzzles, things requiring solutions. Hanging out became exercises, tests, theories. The closer he got to someone, the further away the idea of them became. He built walls without even meaning to. Brick by brick, layer by layer, until he couldn't see them anymore. Couldn't hear them anymore. Sealed away, he moved on to new ideas. Consuming everything in his path. These people, these names, they were a constant in his life and he was grateful for them. They were a hi and hello, never a "how are you?" or a "How's Harvey?" No one cared about Harvey. No one asked about Harvey. No one knew about Harvey.

"Hello, friends." He greeted them, his tone a happy cadence. He felt better about everything as a whole. Harvey wasn't coming home tonight, or tomorrow night but that was okay. He needed his space and Mike was gonna give it to him. He was going to make sure Harvey found the peace he needed. Someone had to. And that was what they all should be concerned with, whether or not Harvey was at peace. Hadn't they all suffered enough? But then, something shifted, something changed within him. He felt it as one would process seeing a bad omen. It settled in his frame, making itself comfortable in the cages of his bones. They would never find peace. Not together, not like this.

Hours passed without Mike moving from that spot. He found himself meditating quietly in the dark room, never having started a game, never having disconnected, merely taking off his headset and laying it at his feet, his eyes staring at the floor in front of him.

The anxiety he felt was centered between his shoulder blades and radiated into his neck, a painful ache, a squelched scream of nerves. He couldn't pull away from the feeling of impending doom that enveloped him. It held him fast to one spot, rooted in fear and agitation. This was real life. This was reality. There was going to be a tomorrow and a next week and a next month and someday they were going to be old and have to account for their lives. Have to look back and see what they'd done. He hated the thought. Wrinkles, gray hair, decaying muscles, soon they'd all be like Sam. Soon they'd all look like Sam. And what were they doing? Cleaning the apartment over and over again? Replacing dishes because they couldn't be bothered to wash them in a timely manner?

Is this what Aurora meant when she said they were running out of time? That she wanted more out of life? Had he gotten it wrong this whole time? Somewhere, deep within himself, Mike felt the tug.

'It's time.'

The fear pressed harder on his shoulders. It wasn't time. It couldn't have been time. But the pull was more insistent. Not going anywhere. Not doing anything. It was time. There was nothing he could do to stop it. Everything he was had been leading up to this moment. This was the point of his creation. This was what he was born to be. Born to do. Born to die.

'It's time.'

He went to the fridge and pulled out a beer. He needed something more. Something bigger. Something that could let him disconnect just enough. Just disconnect. Just turn off. Is this what it all came down to? Did it have to be him? *Did it have to be him?* He gulped the beer down and went for another. It was cold and it tasted terrible. The anxiety didn't dissipate. He bounced on the balls of his feet, pulsating. He grabbed the pack of cigarettes on the kitchen counter and lit one, inside, outside, didn't matter anymore. Nothing mattered. It was time. His whole life had been leading to this moment.

Beer three. Beer four. Beer five. Beer six. Beer seven. Beer eight. All in the same spot, one right after another. His body rocked against the sink and he sunk down to the floor. It was time. It was time. It was time. It was time. It was time. It was time. It was time. It was time. It was time.

Beer nine. Beer ten. Beer eleven. Beer twelve. Beer thirteen. It only seemed to build the feeling. Intensify it. He let an anguished cry rip through his lips. Didn't they realize that's all he was ever trying to do was save them? Didn't they know he was just doing the best he could with what he was given?

He stumbled to the bathroom, swallowing the sick feeling rising in his gut, he needed something. He needed someone. He shouldn't be alone. They couldn't survive alone. Not like this. Not on their own.

How he got the phone in his hands, he didn't know. A short list of names with the singular most important one at the top. He couldn't focus. But he had to do something. Had to do this. Had to speak to her. Had to hear her voice. Had to know it was over. Had to know there was no hope. It was time.

"Hello?" Her feminine voice sounded so far away, so disconnected from where he was.

"Aurora." He said slowly, he wasn't sure where he was anymore. Holding a phone. Laying in a bathtub. Somewhere he had the realization that there was blood oozing out of cuts on his arm. The feeling gave new meaning to the phrase 'razor burn.'

"Where'd those come from?" He asked out loud, only slightly aware of the phone he was still holding.

"Harvey?" The voice on the other end sounded more quizzical than concerned.

"Aurora." Mike licked his lips, trying to concentrate. But all he could see were the thin lines starting at his shoulder and moving closer to the crook of his elbow, stopping just short of a large green vein. "I'm bleeding, Aurora."

There was a pause on the other end, then she knew him. Put pieces together like the wonderous woman she'd always been. Didn't need to see to know, "Mike, you have Harvey's phone again."

"Why am I bleeding, Aurora? Why'd I do that?" He asked, his head swaying back and forth. He needed to get something. Get something for the blood.

"Mike, what's going on?" She asked, her voice sounding strangely concerned.

"I'm fine." He whispered, "I just needed to talk to you."

"Where are you bleeding?" Aurora asked, her tone still off. Still different. Still worried. That wasn't right. She didn't need to be worried. No one had to be worried. He was fine. He was fine. He was fine. He was fine.

"I'm fine, Aurora." He repeated, "I'm fine."

"Are you drunk, Mike?"

"Only a little." His head found a resting place against the side of the bathtub. His eyes rolled backwards for a second and he momentarily lost consciousness, forcefully, he pulled himself back to the land of the living. "Why'd you leave us, Aurora?" He asked.

"I don't think we should talk about this right now, Mike." She sounded… pained. Emotionally weary.

"We miss you." He pressed onwards, "We need you. Harvey needs you."

"Mike, I can't talk about this right now." She was going to hang up, he could feel it. But she was the only thing keeping him rooted to the land of the living. He needed her.

"Please don't go." He whispered.

"Mike, I have to. We have rules. You have to follow them. I thought this was an emergency." She was bothered. He was bothering her. He was always bothering her.

"It's not an emergency." He whispered, "I'll have Sam call you later."

He hung up the phone. He was always making the mistakes. He was always doing the wrong thing. Sam wouldn't be calling her. Hopefully no one would be calling her. They weren't rule breakers. They respected her autonomy.

Caregiver fatigue.

Part Five:
Sunday
.A.Less.Sad.Sam.

Things aren't right, Sam.
Things aren't right at home, Sam.

A year ago.

The rubber pieces on the bottom of Sam's yellow socks gripped the floor as he paced to and fro. So they were here again. Here. Again. The synthetic white light from the rectangular fixture in his room illuminated the white walls, his thin linens laid in a crumpled mess at the foot of his bed, he thought about laying down. He would look more normal if he could just stop moving. He would look more approachable. He would look more like Harvey.

"Be more like Harvey." He muttered, agitated. But the body, it wanted to move, it wanted to act. He dropped into a lunge, the stiff cotton fibers of the blue scrubs he was wearing pulled in all the wrong places. He was doing this wrong. He did a set of walking lunges across the length of the room to the door. He turned on his heels and repeated the process to the opposite side of the wall.

There was a tentative knock at the door. Sam straightened up, he faced the door as it slowly opened, a gentle looking nurse was holding a plastic cup full of broken chalk pieces, "we thought you might like to draw."

She had dark hair, pulled into a bun, her heart shaped face accentuated with soft, almond shaped dark eyes. Her mouth looked like it spent a lot of time smiling.

Sam blinked, it took him half a moment to process what she was saying, he'd forgotten there was a wall set up to look like a chalkboard next to him, he hadn't seen it as important. It wasn't important. He didn't want to draw, he wanted to go home and in order to go home he had to pretend to stabilize.

Mike's charming smile spread across his face, he felt his posture relax and his eyebrows let go of their frown, it was easily done. Easily practiced, easily rehearsed, "thanks, that would be nice, I think I'm going stir crazy," he mustered a chuckle. Easily practiced, easily rehearsed.

But maybe 'stir crazy' wasn't the right thing to say, she looked nervous, like her words and actions were on their tip toes, testing out the layers of ice on a freshly frozen lake.

"How are you feeling this morning?" She asked, never fully stepping into the room, cradling the cup of chalk with both hands.

"A little frustrated." He sighed, "With myself."

She nodded sympathetically, "Yeah, it's been a rough week for you, hasn't it, Harvey?"

Internally Sam winced, it'd been a whole week? They'd been here a week? Where'd he been? What'd he been doing? Maybe she just meant in general. Maybe it was a figure of expression. Surely he hadn't been here an entire week. He had a work schedule he had to follow.

"Yeah," He matched her tone and energy in the conversation, he had to be Harvey and Harvey had to know what was going on, "It's just hard."

"Well, the doctor will be by later today to see you, to see how you're doing and assess everything." There was light positivity in her voice now, that was a good sign.

He didn't know how he should respond to that, should he sound happy about it? Should the fact, that in reality brought him anxiety, be a positive one? Did he want to speak to a doctor? No. He wanted to go home. But that meant he had to speak to someone. Had to convince them that everyone, *everything*, was fine. He was fine.

"That's good." He nodded, "I'll take the chalk, it'll help me pass the time."

She smiled, "good! I'll just leave it right here for you."

She set it down just inside the room and her hand clasped the handle of the door, retreating quickly, swinging the door closed just enough that it was left barely cracked open. The illusion of privacy.

Sam stared at the chalkboard wall with a piece of chalk in his hand, he was not creative. He didn't care for drawing. But he mustered a doodle and built off of it. Abstract shapes that looked like they could be a creative art piece. He didn't want to be here forever.

Present Sunday

Sam was awake. His left arm stung and his neck was sore. Again, he was waking up in the bathtub. Why were they always in the fucking bathtub?

He pulled his weary frame to a sitting position and his woozy, hung over, head wobbled on his shoulders. His stomach clenched and he felt the intense urge to vomit. It was while he was bent over the toilet that he noticed the actual state of his arm. Thin, red, razor blade cuts that'd mostly dried overnight. A couple deeper ones still held a healthy sheen to them where the blood wasn't quite done drying, only partially congealed.

He did his best to expel the lack of contents from his stomach and flushed the toilet before falling backwards into a defeated sitting position, looking and not looking at his arm. Taking stock in the state of everything.

Harvey's phone laid a few feet away from him and Sam reached for it, pulling up the call log. Two minutes with Aurora on the phone around 3 a.m. That was Mike. Which meant the rest of everything else was Mike. Which meant things were definitely escalating. Devolving. Breaking down.

Sam needed to take a shower before he did anything else. He knew what was about to happen, he knew how this all played out and he needed to be freshly showered to save them from any more embarrassment.

It's time.

Oh, Harvey, you dear boy. It's been time for a long time.

Sam got to his feet and rummaged around for fresh clothes. He laid a towel on the floor in front of the tub for his feet and hung another up on the shower curtain rod. He took his time in the shower, slowly, methodically, washing away what he could of the evidence. Afterwards, he brushed his teeth three times and gargled the mouthwash till his cheeks and gums burned.

They were done fighting him. They were done attempting to pretend. Attempting to fake it till they made it. He was going to be allowed to do what he needed to do.

As he cleaned up Mike's mess from the night before, Harvey's phone, which was now securely in his back pocket, started to vibrate.

He closed his eyes and drew in a deep breath. It was time.

"Hello?" He answered, knowing that if things were going to get better, he'd have to make this first step in a long line of steps.

"Harvey?" the maternal voice of the woman who raised him came through.

"I'm here." Harvey's despondent, yet clear tone responded.

"Aurora called me this morning," his mom continued, "She's worried about you. She said she thinks you hurt yourself last night."

Harvey nodded without replying, that's definitely what happened. Was there any going back? Any way to undo this moment? Could he start the week over? Just pretend. Just put a fake voice on and pretend.

It's time, Harvey.

Harvey let himself sit in silence for a few seconds before he cleared his throat, "I need help, mom."